Lots of Lights

For more information and books on Indian culture, please
visit http://www.maharanimamas.com/

Inspired by my little Hati's
Anik & Aryana.
You light up my life

Pratham USA
Every child in School and Learning Well

Namaste. My name is Ram
and this is my sister Saanvi

Everyone is humming
because Diwali is coming.
What is Diwali? you ask

Mama says,
Diwali is similar to Hanukkah
but without the yamaka
and feels like Christmas glee
but without the big tree

Papa calls it the festival of light
where everything shines bright

Nani and Nanaji say
it is the start of the New Year
so fill your heart with cheer

Dadi and Dadaji say
it is the celebration of inner light
that keeps us doing things right

It is five days of fun for
everyone
"How do we celebrate?
you ask"

Day 1: Dhan Teras
We clean and cook
and read this Diwali book.
We put up a special tent
where we each get a present.

We make a Rangoli by
decorating the floor
next to the door with
colors galore.

Day 2: Choti Diwali

We decorate diyas to put
in each room.
This is a special rite we do at night
under the full moon.

Outside we string lights
at different heights
much to our neighbors
wonder and delight

This week we are excited
to see the house lighted.

Day 3: Diwali
We wake up early and rush
to the tent
to see what gifts we have been sent.

Later that day
we sit down to pray
to the goddess of wealth
for prosperity and health

We watch as rockets shoot up high
to make beautiful fireworks in the sky

Day 4: Annakut
We wake up late for
a brunch date.
The whole family enjoys
a big feast
till Papa's pant button
is released

Day 5: Bhai Dooj

This is a special day
for Saanvi and me to play
She uses powder that is red
to put a tikka on my head.
We hug and promise mother
to try not to bug each other

Now that you know all
about Diwali

Please accept our humble invite

to celebrate with us the festival of light.

Diya

Rangoli

Kandils

Diwali Mubarak: Happy Diwali

Tohfa

Pooja

Mitha

Explore the meaning of Indian words in this story you do not know

Explanation of Diwali for Parents

Diwali is often referred to as the "festival of lights" and compared to New Years or Christmas. Diwali is celebrated on different dates in different parts of India. It is a time for family and friends to share music, gifts, fireworks and prayer. Across India, Diwali is celebrated for different reasons, but spiritually it is "the awareness of the inner light". The celebration of Diwali as the "victory of good over evil", refers to the light of higher knowledge dispelling all ignorance and the awareness of the oneness of all things.

CPSIA information can be obtained at www.ICGtesting.com
Printed in the USA
LVIW01n2310100117
520513LV00006B/21